TOMATOES IN MY LUNCHBOX

WRITTEN BY
Costantia Manoli

ILLUSTRATED BY
Magdalena Mora

ROARING BROOK PRESS
New York

I don't recognize my name at roll call the first time.

The teacher says it like it's too hard to understand.
Then she says it again, one syllable at a time. It's strange
and sharp, and sounds like something is breaking.

Then children in my class say my name,
and it is like it doesn't fit in their mouths.
It sounds like a question every time.

Emily   Robin
Andrew   Marcus
Maria   Kwota
Jackie
Terrence
Carlos
Iris

When my mama says my name, it's soft like summer
and round with love and color and light.

I want to be Olivia, Sophie, or Chloe.
Or Emma, with yellow hair like the
sun and the blue sky in her eyes—
any other name that is an answer.
They can laugh and dance, and
everyone understands their names.

My mama tells me my name is beautiful and it's different.
But it's not beautiful here, and I don't want to be different.

I want a name that fits inside the front of my book.
I want a name I say once and people know it's a name.

I want a name that stories are about.

When we came here, we left the place where my name fit. We took what we could and closed it in our suitcases . . .

Our things look weird here.
My clothes are weird here.
The whole tomato in my lunchbox is weird here.

I bite into it, and the insides spurt out.
It tastes like home . . .

but I have to spend the rest of the
day with those stains on my shirt.

Mama tells me I just need to make some new friends.
That's all.
But I don't know how . . .

I pick an Emma, and I try to be like her.
I go where she goes. I do what she does.
I say what she says.

It doesn't work.
If my name were Emma, too, we'd have
something to smile to each other about,
and we could share secrets.

But I'm not an Emma. It doesn't fit me.

There is a whole world in my name.
I carry it with me. It's heavy carrying
your whole world around with you all
the time.

Grandma says a smile can lighten a heavy load.
I smile at Chloe. I want to smile a big, sunshiny
smile, but it ends up being small. Chloe asks,
"Where's your name from, anyway?"

I shrug and say, "It was my grandmother's name." But my voice wobbles a bit, so I don't say much more.

I don't tell her it belonged to the person I loved most.
The person I left behind in a place that shines with
yellow sun and with blue, blue skies. The place where
our names are familiar and beautiful . . .

The memory makes my smile
big and sunshiny, though.

Chloe nods and smiles back.

The following day, I sit next to her in class.
She doesn't speak during the lesson, but
when it's time to leave, she points at my
scarf and says, "Yellow is my favorite color."

I whisper, "It's my favorite color, too."
I've never told anyone here that before.

I wear yellow all the time after that. So does she.

On the day she forgets her lunch, I offer her mine to share. She smiles and takes it like I'm giving her a gift.

We sit with tomato seeds on our shirts and talk and talk, and it's like a door opening. We laugh and dance under the shining sun and skies so blue.

Later, we say hello to Olivia and Sophie.
Chloe tells us a story, and my name is in it.
It sounds soft and round and full of color
as she says it with pride.

My friends say it again in turns, and my name is not a question anymore. It is familiar and gentle and beautiful.
It is all in one piece and . . .

it sounds like home.

AUTHOR'S NOTE

Costantia is not an easy name to say in English. It's long and it's awkward and it sounds quite a bit different from the way you might read it.

There were no *Costantias* around when I was growing up. I lived in London and went to an English primary school and was therefore mostly surrounded by English teachers and English children who struggled with my name. So, my long and soft-sounding Cypriot name very quickly became a more manageable clipped and shortened version. In some ways it was a relief; Tina, Tia, Connie, and Cozie were (and in many cases still are!) far easier alternatives to use. It did make life a bit simpler for me, not having to explain my name over and over again. However, I would always feel anxiety and dread ball up in my stomach when a teacher would read my name from a list for the first time, or when I met someone new who would ask, "What's your name?" I always worried that I'd make people feel uncomfortable if I replied with a name they couldn't easily pronounce. In Greek, my name simply rolls off the tongue. Consonant sounds are softer and longer; *Costantia* in English becomes *Goh-stahn-DEE-yah* in Greek. As I said, it sounds quite a bit different from the way you might read it!

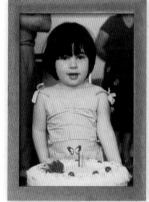

Me on my third birthday in our London home

My sister, Paula, and I in front of the Landseer Lions at Trafalgar Square

Walker School photo

So, when you have a name that even *you* can't say in English, AND your mom puts things in your lunchbox like whole tomatoes (the big ones, not cute little ones that you can pop into your mouth), it's easy to feel like you are different.

I remember watching the other children at school with their neat and delicate white bread sandwiches, cut into perfect squares and triangles, and the latest snacks and treats that I'd seen advertised on TV and so desperately wanted to try. My lunchbox was different. There would have been other things in there to accompany the tomato, but all I remember now is that—the whole tomato that I bit into like an apple and the seeds that decorated my school pinafore after. It was comforting to have something that was so clearly a connection to home; my mom is a fantastic cook, and tomatoes—usually chopped and peeled, sometimes pureed, other times layered or stuffed—form the basis of many favorite Cypriot dishes that she prepared for us at home back then . . . and she still does now!

It can take time to discover what is in a name. It can take time to understand why our parents gift us with the names they do, where they have come

Paula and I with Pappou Costa in London
(I'm on the left)

from, and what the name means. *Costantia* means constancy—steadfastness, loyalty, determination. It has always been a reminder of where my family comes from, because when you grow up somewhere different, it can be easy to forget that. It is a connection to the grandfather I was named after and the generations that came before. Even more than that, it is mine. It has become a part of me, and now I, too, am the story of my name.

For the ones who named me
and the two I named myself
—C. M.

For Esther and Magdaleno
—M. M.

Published by Roaring Brook Press
Roaring Brook Press is a division of Holtzbrinck Publishing Holdings Limited Partnership
120 Broadway, New York, NY 10271 · mackids.com

Text copyright © 2022 by Costantia Manoli
Illustrations copyright © 2022 by Magdalena Mora
All rights reserved.

Our books may be purchased in bulk for promotional, educational, or business use.
Please contact your local bookseller or the Macmillan Corporate and Premium Sales Department
at (800) 221-7945 ext. 5442 or by email at MacmillanSpecialMarkets@macmillan.com.

Library of Congress Cataloging-in-Publication Data is available.

First edition, 2022
The art for this book was rendered using inks, pastels, water-soluble crayons, and digital collage.
The type face is Goby. The book was edited by Connie Hsu, designed by Mercedes Padró, and art directed by Aram
Kim. The production was managed by Susan Doran, and the production editor was Kathy Wielgosz.

Printed in China by Hung Hing Off-set Printing Co. Ltd., Heshan City, Guangdong Province

ISBN 978-1-250-76312-9
1 3 5 7 9 10 8 6 4 2